PRINCESS Mariana AND LIXO ISLAND

INAUGURAL SERIES: STORY 3
OF THE
GUARDIAN PRINCESSES

This book was produced by the collective work of the Guardian Princess Alliance.

Written by Ashanti McMillon

Editorial Assistance:
Setsu Shigematsu
Ilse Ackerman
Kelsey Moore
Rié Collett
Ron Collett
Nausheen Sheikh
Pachet Bryant

Illustrated by A. Das
Preliminary sketches by Dalia Quiroz, Kayla Madison, and Michelle Le
Wardrobe design by Kayla Madison, Sophia Wu, and Nausheen Sheikh

Cover and layout by Vikram Sangha
Common Core questions and activity by Tracy Hualde
Reading level assessment by Candice Herron

ISBN: 978-0-9913194-2-8
Library of Congress Control Number: 2013957497

GUARDIAN
PRINCESSES

PRINCESS
Mariana
AND
LIXO ISLAND

WRITTEN BY
ASHANTI McMILLON
& THE GUARDIAN PRINCESS ALLIANCE

ILLUSTRATED BY A. DAS

ONCE UPON A TIME there was a smart and caring princess named Mariana. She lived in the kingdom of Armonía. It was a beautiful island with tall palm trees, warm sands, and an abundance of fruit trees. Princess Mariana was the Guardian of the Seas. She could talk to all of the sea creatures, from the tiniest seahorses to the biggest blue whales. Every day, she would run to the beach and swim with her sea friends to explore the ocean. Princess Mariana would sing:

El Mar is our magnificent home
With endless waves where we can roam
Clear blue seas shimmering in the sun
A place where sea creatures can all have fun
A home with joy and energy
A place where we can all be free
We love the agua, we love the sea
I'll take care of you, as you take care of me

El Mar: Spanish for "the sea"
Agua: Spanish for "water"

The land and sea creatures in the kingdom were called Armonians, and they lived together in perfect harmony. The seas surrounding Armonía were filled with Fulsi fish. Whenever the Fulsi fish were happy, their scales glittered. The sea was so clean and pure that it shimmered from the Fulsis' colorful, shining scales. They could breathe air, walk on land, and make the waves glow with their glittering scales.

A Fulsi fish named Iris was Princess Mariana's best friend. They would go on adventures together, along with their good friend Feliz, the fastest dolphin in the kingdom. Feliz always gave them rides on his back to any part of the ocean that they wished to explore.

One day, Princess Mariana, Iris, and Feliz were in the ocean playing with the sea turtles. As the sea turtles were telling stories about their ancestors, a voice cried from the distance. "HELP! I'm trapped! Someone help me! I can't move!"

Princess Mariana and her friends quickly swam toward the voice and found a seal caught inside a black rubber tire. "This is very dangerous! We must rescue him from that trap!" exclaimed the sea turtle. They all worked together to free the seal.

"Thank you so much," said the exhausted seal. "I was so scared. I was just swimming through the waves, and then suddenly I was caught in this awful trap."

One of the sea turtles said, "That trap is called a tire. It does not belong in the occan. Unfortunately, people litter the oceans every day with tires, garbage, and many other kinds of trash. We have seen how litter, or *basura*, dumped into *El Mar* hurts our friends."

"Yes, litter often traps and harms our sea friends," said the other sea turtle. "We also sometimes think it's food and accidentally eat it, which makes us very sick. Anything that does not belong in the sea is pollution. There are also many islands polluted with litter."

"Something must be done!" exclaimed Princess Mariana. "We cannot have islands covered with litter polluting our beautiful oceans and harming sea creatures! Mr. Seal, where were you swimming?" she asked.

The seal said, "I swam by an island covered with litter. It is called Lixo Island. I can take you to it."

"Yes please! Let's go right away. *¡Vámonos!*" Princess Mariana said.

Basura: Spanish for "garbage"
Vámonos: Spanish for "let's go"

9

They soon arrived at an island covered with garbage and slime. When they saw the island, tears came to their eyes. Princess Mariana and her friends had never seen such waste. It was a horrible place.

Then they heard the sound of footsteps sloshing in the slime. A crowd of dark figures arose from the trash heaps and walked towards them. One of the tall dark figures said, "Who goes there? Who dares to cross the sands of Lixo Island?"

"My name is Princess Mariana, Guardian of the Seas," she said confidently. "I am here with my sea friends to find out why the ocean is being polluted with litter. We came here to stop this from happening!"

The tall dark figure began laughing. "You think you can stop this? Well, you are wrong! My name is Prince Sujo, ruler of the Spumas of Lixo Island. I was appointed by King Abaddon, ruler of Voracity, to be in charge of collecting his kingdom's garbage and waste."

Princess Mariana replied, "There's so much garbage here that it is overflowing into the ocean. Surely not all of these things are waste. Do you know that bottles, cans, and many other things can be recycled and turned into new things? We can help you clean it up."

Prince Sujo walked out of the shadows and said, "This island has too much trash for anyone, even a powerful princess, to remove!" He continued,

"Just look at the old rubber tires by the wilting trees,
with no fruit, few branches, and certainly no leaves.
Broken glass and plastic bags are scattered everywhere,
tattered shoes that no one would ever care to wear.
We have crushed soda cans and six-pack rings,
plastic bottles, Styrofoam, and other disgusting things.
Junk and chunks of compacted trash,
this is where Voracity's waste is stashed."

Princess Mariana responded, "It is wrong for King Abaddon to dump waste on your home. Your people are suffering! Why don't you stand up to him? We can help you." Prince Sujo said, "There is nothing that can be done!" He summoned the other dark figures. "Spumas, tell this princess who you are!"

The slimy and dirty Spumas began to sing:

Spumas! Spumas! That is who we are
We live on a dirty island made from garbage and tar
Spumas! Spumas! We swim in thick black oil
That King Abaddon dumped here, leaving trash to rot and spoil

Prince Sujo turned to the princess and said, "Now, I suggest you leave. You have no business here."

"This island is a danger to you, the Spumas, and all of our sea friends. We shall leave for now but will soon return to Lixo Island. We must keep the waters clean!" Princess Mariana said. She turned away and jumped on Feliz's back, and they returned to Armonía.

As they approached Armonía Island, Princess Mariana noticed that the Fulsi fish were no longer glowing. The *basura* in the water was making them all sick. Iris said, "Princess, we are not happy. We must find a way to remove this litter soon or else the glowing power of the Fulsi fish will be lost for good."

Princess Mariana paced back and forth as she pondered what to do. *I need help from my friends*, she thought, so she sent three messenger birds asking her friends to come quickly.

The next morning, Princess Mariana heard the sound of a strong gust of wind. She ran outside and saw Princess Terra, Princess Vinnca, and Princess Ten Ten descending on a cloud.

Princess Mariana exclaimed, "Thank you for coming, friends! I really need your help!" She told them about how King Abaddon had turned Lixo Island into a wasteland. She explained how its trash was spreading across the sea to Armonía and beyond.

Princess Terra said, "I know about King Abaddon's dirty deeds. He must be stopped."

Princess Vinnea nodded. "Yes. We have to get rid of this pollution. But how?"

"We can work together to remove the garbage from Lixo Island," Princess Mariana said. Then she began explaining her plan…

The next day, Princess Mariana and her friends arrived at Lixo Island. A big ship with "VORACITY WASTE" printed on its side was docked by the shore. The Spumas were unloading the trash from the ship and throwing it onto the island.

Princess Mariana called out, "Prince Sujo, where are you? We are back!"

Prince Sujo walked off the ship and sneered, "Oh, look at what we have here. What do you want now?"

"My friends and I have come to get rid of the *basura* on this island," she responded.

Prince Sujo laughed. "That's impossible. You are foolish for trying."

The Spumas marched toward the princesses and chanted:

> *We are the Spumas*
> *Covered in dirt and grime*
> *Listen to Prince Sujo, and hear our rhyme*
> *It is impossible for you to clean this place*
> *The mess is everywhere, even on our face*
> *You can't clean this mess or stop it from smelling*
> *Just give up now and go back to your dwelling*

The princesses stood their ground and began to carry out their plan.

Princess Mariana began to blow through her favorite conch shell. The sound echoed across the sea, summoning her sea friend, Humberto, the big blue whale.

Princess Ten Ten, Guardian of the Skies, flew towards the clouds and began to create a big gust of wind, singing:

Mighty winds come and go
Lift the dirty trash below

As the trash began whirling into the sky, Princess Terra, Guardian of the Land, knelt down, touched the black sand, and sang:

Dear precious Earth, heal this sand
Bring forth the clean and natural land

The black oil covering the sands rose and floated into Princess Ten Ten's wind ball. The sand was now sparkling clean. Meanwhile, Princess Mariana, Guardian of the Seas, stood in the slimy dark waters. She closed her eyes and sang:

Tides that ebb and flow, push and pull
Let these waters become clean, and the color azul

The sludge and slime lifted from the ocean and swirled into the wind ball. The ocean was now clean and bright blue. Then, from deep beneath the waves, Humberto rose to the surface. "Bring in the water!" Princess Mariana told the whale. From his blowhole, he began to shoot sea water high into the air. Princess Ten Ten motioned a big gust of wind to blow the water onto the trees to clean them.

Then, Princess Vinnea, Guardian of Plant Life, walked over and touched one of the trees. She closed her eyes and sang:

Tree to tree, fruits come alive
Vine to vine, plant life be revived

Azul: Spanish for "blue"

The rotten food that was still lying on the sands sank beneath the moist ground. Suddenly, the plants and trees started to grow bright green leaves. Coconuts, mangoes, and pineapples appeared. The island now looked as bountiful as Armonía. "How are you doing this?!" Prince Sujo screamed.

"Prince Sujo, now it's time for you and the Spumas to get cleaned up too!" Princess Mariana said. She took an empty shell and used it to scoop the clean ocean water. She began to sing:

Spumas, Spumas
Dirty on the outside, feeling you're all alone
You're pure on the inside, there's beauty in your corazón!

The grime covering Prince Sujo and the Spumas disappeared, revealing Prince Sujo to be a fine young man and the Spumas to be good people with kind faces. As soon as they were clean, the Spumas began to help pick up the remaining litter on the beaches.

The princesses took the litter from the Spumas and magically turned it into new, useful things. The broken glass became colorful tiles and bowls. The plastic turned into beach toys and beach chairs. The shredded paper turned into pretty lanterns. Meanwhile, the waste contained in the wind ball spun faster and faster until it burst into sparkles that made Lixo Island shine.

Corazón: Spanish for "heart"

King Abaddon's sailors were shocked by how the princess and her companions cleaned the island. Humberto knocked the side of the ship to get the sailors' attention. They were scared by the presence of the big blue whale.

"That's Humberto's way of saying don't pollute our ocean again," Princess Mariana said. "Tell King Abaddon that we are here to protect the sea and all of its marine life." The sailors nodded in fear and awe and quickly sailed back to Voracity as fast as they could.

The Spumas cheered and ran up to the princesses and their sea friends. Prince Sujo said, "We thank you and your friends, Princess Mariana. My real name is Prince Amel. My kingdom was taken over by the greedy King Abaddon when I was a child. He cast a spell on our home and turned it into Lixo Island. We were turned into dirty Spumas."

He continued, "We have been serving him for years not realizing the harm we were causing. You and your friends are true heroes for helping us clean our island and our ocean!"

"You are welcome, Prince Amel," Princess Mariana said, "but our magic alone is not enough. We all must do our part to keep the islands and oceans clean."

Smiling with gratitude, Prince Amel agreed and said, "From this day forth, our home shall be called Renova Island, and my people, Renovians. We will work to keep our home and beaches clean. We will recycle *basura* to take care of the Earth."

"That sounds like the start of a great plan," said Princess Ten Ten.

"In honor of you and your friends, let's have our first celebration as Renova Island today. How does that sound?" asked Prince Amel. Everyone cheered.

That afternoon, they all gathered at the beach. They sang songs and ate the freshly grown fruit. The sea turtles told old stories to the young guppies. Feliz and the other dolphins played in the waves and leaped in the air. The waters of Renova Island were now glowing from the happy Fulsi fish. They all played games and danced.

The Guardian Princesses shared their pledge with Prince Amel and the Renovians.

We pledge to do what is just and fair
To do our best to protect and care
For all living beings great and small have worth
We shall come together to take care of our Earth
We'll care for the ocean and the beauty of the sea
So marine life can flourish, be happy and free
We shall protect the seas, skies, and lands of all nations
To be cherished and shared by the next generations

The End

ETYMOLOGY CHART

Etymology: the history of a word

Name	Language	Meaning
Amel	Arabic	hope, derived from Amal
Armonía	Latin/Spanish	joint, agreement; harmony (pronounced ar·mo·NEE·ah)
Feliz	Latin/Portuguese	happy; derived from the Latin word Felix
Fulsi	Latin	shines
Iris	Greek/Latin	rainbow
Lixo	Latin/Portuguese	garbage; waste (pronounced LEE·shoo)
Mariana	Hebrew Latin	related to Mary/Maria; associated with *stella maris*, star of the sea
Renova	Latin/Portuguese	renews; restores
Spuma	Latin	foam, slime
Sujo	Portuguese	dirty (pronounced SOO·zhoo)

GLOSSARY

Ancestors: people who are related to you who lived a long time ago

Bountiful: large in quantity; plentiful

Conch shell: the shell of a type of tropical mollusk that is usually brightly colored with a spiral shape; it may be used as a type of wind instrument

Harmony: to be in agreement; to have a peaceful, friendly relationship

Marine life: plants and animals that live in the oceans, lakes, and rivers

Pollution: putting unclean, dirty, or harmful things that don't belong somewhere in an environment (for example, smog is a kind of air pollution)

Ponder: to carefully think about something

Recycle: to make something new from something that has been used before; to process used objects (for example, glass, cans, or paper) into new material

Waste: material left over, rejected, or thrown away

COMMON CORE DISCUSSION QUESTIONS

Designed for 3rd grade reading level.

1. Describe Princess Mariana. Be sure to provide page numbers as evidence to support your answers. What is her role as a Guardian Princess? (RL.3.1)

2. The setting is important to this story. Look closely at the illustrations and read Mariana's first song again on page 4. Find at least three words or phrases that describe the ocean and why it is important as a setting. (RL.3.1, RL.3.7)

3. Reread the part of the story when Princess Mariana rescues the seal on page 8. The author states on page 9, "We have seen how litter, or *basura,* dumped into *El Mar* has hurt our friends." What does "*basura*" mean? What word could you use to replace it? (RL.3.4, L.3.4) List at least three problems that *basura* is causing. Provide evidence. (RL.3.1)

4. Reread the section of the story when Princess Mariana meets Prince Sujo and the Spumas for the first time on Lixo Island on pages 10-14. Now reread the part when Princess Mariana transforms them on pages 24-27. How do the feelings, actions, and even the names of these characters change as the story progresses? (RL.3.1, RL.3.3, RL. 3.5)

5. What are Fulsi fish? How does Lixo Island impact them? (RL.3.1, RL.3.7)

6. *Princess Mariana and Lixo Island* is the first book in the series to have four princesses working together. Describe how the actions of each princess help change Lixo Island. (RL.3.3)

7. What is the author's central message or lesson in *Princess Mariana and Lixo Island*? Be sure to use key details throughout the story to prove your thinking. (RL.3.2)

COMMON CORE ACTIVITY

Towards the end of the story, Princess Mariana says:

**"…our magic alone is not enough. We all must do our part
to keep the islands and oceans clean."** (page 26)

Write a paragraph about keeping the oceans clean. Include at least two specific details explaining what you can do and a concluding statement. (W.3.2a, W.3.2b, W.3.2d)